DATE DUE

Motocross Tricks

Janey Levy

PowerKiDS press™

New York

To Tyrone, for his patience and for teaching me about motor sports

Published in 2007 by The Rosen Publishing Group, Inc.
29 East 21st Street, New York, NY 10010

First Edition

Editor: Joanne Randolph
Book Design: Ginny Chu
Layout Design: Kate Laczynski

Photo Credits: Cover, pp. 1, 5–8, 10–15, 17, 21–23, 25–26, 28–29 © Simon Cudby Photo; p. 19 © Robert Cianflone/Allsport/Getty Images.

Library of Congress Cataloging-in-Publication Data

Levy, Janey.
    Motocross tricks / Janey Levy. — 1st ed.
        p. cm. — (Motocross)
    Includes index.
    ISBN-13: 978-1-4042-3697-4 (library binding)
    ISBN-10: 1-4042-3697-X (library binding)
    1. Motocross—Juvenile literature. I. Title.
    GV1060.12.L49 2007
    796.7'56—dc22
                                                    2006032994

Manufactured in the United States of America

Contents

Death-Defying Tricks

Freestyle motocross (freestyle MX or FMX) is motocross's newest form. Motocross (MX) is a type of motorcycle racing run on dirt tracks in country areas. The tracks have hills, twists, turns, man-made jumps, rhythm sections, whoops, and tabletops. Supercross and Arenacross are motocross races run on man-made dirt tracks in stadiums or arenas. Sometimes riders in these races perform tricks. However, the big place for tricks is freestyle MX.

Freestyle has two main types of events, freestyle MX and big air, or best trick. In freestyle MX riders do several short runs on a course with take-off ramps and landing ramps. They perform astounding tricks while flying between the ramps. In big air each rider performs a single trick three times.

Professional riders can make astounding tricks look easy. However, the tricks are actually very hard and dangerous. Even top riders have been seriously hurt

Here a freestyle rider does a Double Superman Seat Grab during the 2006 X Games.

Besides the X Games, the X-Fighters competitions are some of the best in the world. The top U.S. freestyle riders hope to be invited to these competitions, which are held in bullfighting rings.

many times while learning and performing tricks. Anyone who wants to perform tricks must first learn to ride well, then start with the easiest tricks. He or she must wear safety gear and practice a lot.

The Nac-Nac is one of freestyle's original tricks. It started out as a trick used in bicycle motocross

Jeff Alessi does a Nac-Nac. Every freestyle rider learns how to do this trick.

(BMX). Supercross champion Jeremy McGrath was the first to perform it in a motocross event. He performed it during a Supercross race in 1994. Fans were wowed and freestyle started to grow. The Nac-Nac became McGrath's signature trick.

The Nac-Nac is simpler than many other tricks, but that does not mean it is easy. In a Nac-Nac the rider acts as if he or she is going to get off the motorcycle while flying through the air! As the rider

7

Kenny Bartram is about to swing his leg back across the seat to finish his Nac-Nac.

flies off the take-off
ramp, he or she leans
forward and lifts one foot
off the foot peg. While
standing on the other
foot, the rider then
swings the leg he or she
lifted off the foot peg over
the rear fender to the opposite side of the machine.
The rider's entire body is now on one side of the
machine. The rider must then swing the leg back
over the rear fender, place the foot back on the foot
peg, and sit down before landing.

The Heel Clicker

The Heel Clicker is another basic trick. The rider lifts both feet off the foot pegs, lifts them up and over the handlebars, and clicks his or her heels together.

The Whip

The Whip is another early freestyle trick. The motorcycle is turned sideways and laid flat while flying through the air.

To perform the trick, the rider whips the rear end of the motorcycle to one side or the other so the machine is flying sideways. Then he or she lays the machine flat on its side. The rider must get the machine upright and pointed straight ahead again before landing.

Here Australian motocross and Supercross rider Chad Reed practices a Whip.

Riders often add other elements to a basic trick to make the trick harder. Sometimes they lift both feet off the foot pegs. Sometimes they hang on to the handlebars, lift their whole body off the machine, and turn around to look behind them! Sometimes they stand on the seat while still holding the handlebars!

The Suicide Whip

In one variation of the Whip, the rider takes his or her hands off the handlebars. This means he or she has no control of the machine. Because some people think this trick is suicidal, the trick is known as the Suicide Whip.

The Superman Seat Grab

The Superman Seat Grab is a more challenging trick. Carey Hart invented the trick, which is a variation of the Superman.

In the Superman the rider lifts both feet off the foot pegs and throws his or her legs out behind the machine so he or she looks like Superman flying through the air. In the Superman Seat Grab, the rider then lets go of the handlebars with one hand and reaches back to grasp

Mike Metzger does a Double Superman Seat Grab. Metzger is one of the creators of freestyle MX.

one of the grab holes in the seat. This makes the rider's legs extend farther back behind the machine.

Carey Hart also invented the Double Superman Seat Grab. In this trick the rider lets go of the handlebars with both hands, slides back, and grasps the seat grab holes with both hands!

Jeremy Stenberg does a Double Superman Seat Grab during the X Games. Stenberg is known for his style when performing tricks.

Carey Hart does a Superman Seat Grab. Hart was the first person to do a backflip on a 250cc motocross machine.

The Cliffhanger

The Cliffhanger is an even scarier trick. One author wrote that the trick requires a rider's handlebars, feet, and all his guts, or bravery. In the Cliffhanger riders stand straight up with their feet hooked under the handlebars and their arms raised above their head.

As soon as the rider leaves the take-off ramp, he or she rises up off the seat, takes both feet off the foot pegs, and brings them up under the handlebars. Then the rider takes his or her hands off the handlebars, stands up, and raises both arms above his or her head. The rider tries to stand as straight as possible and have his or her body right above the handlebars. Then the rider must sit down, grab the handlebars, and get both feet on the foot pegs before landing.

The Cliffhanger is not a trick for the faint of heart. Jeremy Stenberg has no fear, though.

The Lazy Boy

Travis Pastrana invented the Lazy Boy. It is a challenging and popular trick that many riders like to perform in competition. The rider lies back on the seat and sticks his or her legs out in front of the motorcycle.

The Coffin

A trick that is very similar to the Lazy Boy is the Coffin. It is performed the same way except for one difference. The rider keeps his or her hands on the handlebars.

To perform the Lazy Boy, the rider takes both feet off the foot pegs, raises them, and sticks them out in front of the machine under the handlebars. He or she then lies back on the seat, lets go of the handlebars, and reaches both arms back over his or her head. The farther the rider extends his or her arms and legs, the better the trick is considered to be.

This rider has his arms and legs stretched as far as he can. He is trying to win extra points as he performs the Lazy Boy in competition.

The Kiss of Death

The Kiss of Death is one of the harder tricks. In this trick the machine is straight up and down, with the rider upside down above it.

Right after leaving the take-off ramp, the rider positions the machine so the front end is up and the back end is down. Then the rider kicks both legs back and up over his or her head, while still holding on to the handlebars. The rider tries to position his or her body so it looks as if he or she is performing a handstand. Then the rider pushes the front end of the machine down, brings both legs back down, and returns his or her feet to the foot pegs. Rider and machine hit the landing ramp in a standard riding position.

You can see from this picture why the Kiss of Death is thought to be one of the hardest freestyle tricks to perform.

The Backflip

One of the hardest freestyle tricks is the backflip. In this trick rider and machine spin backward and turn a complete circle. Riders talked about doing the backflip for a long time, but most thought it was impossible or too dangerous. Then Carey Hart changed everything when he performed one in a competition in 2000. After that everyone had to learn the backflip.

Kenny Bartram does a backflip. Bartram is the first person ever to land a Side Saddle Backflip.

To perform the backflip, the rider begins to push on the foot pegs and pull on the handlebars as soon as he or she has left the take-off ramp. This causes the machine to swing up and over the rider as he or she spins backward. Rider and machine spin completely around in time to hit the landing ramp right side up.

Some Famous Backflips

Jeremy "Twitch" Stenberg performed the world's longest backflip. He traveled 155 feet (47 m)! Mike "The Godfather" Metzger was the first person to perform a backflip over the fountains in front of the Las Vegas hotel named Caesar's Palace.

Making the Backflip Even Harder

As hard as the backflip is, riders have found ways to make it even harder. Sometimes a rider takes one hand off the handlebars during the trick for a One-Handed Backflip. Sometimes a rider takes both hands and both feet off the machine for a No-Handed No-Footed Backflip!

Riders also perform other tricks while they are spinning backward in the backflip. They do tricks such as the Backflip Nac-Nac, in which they perform the Nac-Nac while they are upside down during the backflip. They also perform the Backflip Cliffhanger and the Backflip Lazy Boy. They even perform the Backflip Nac-Nac to Heel Clicker, which adds the Heel Clicker after the Nac-Nac! At the 2006 X Games, Travis Pastrana performed the first Double Backflip!

Beau Bamberg has added a Nac-Nac to this backflip.

The Rock Solid

One of the very hardest tricks is the Rock Solid. In this trick no part of the rider is touching the machine. The rider is stretched out above the machine, and the two are flying through the air independently!

Kenny Bartram practices the Rock Solid before the start of the X Games competition.

To perform the Rock Solid, the rider starts by doing a Double Superman Seat Grab. Then he or she lets go of the seat completely and extends both arms straight out to the sides! At this point rider and machine are flying through the air completely separate from each other. The rider must then grab the seat again and pull himself or herself back onto the machine before reaching the landing ramp.

Freestyle MX is a popular and exciting sport. New tricks are being created all the time. Riders are limited only by their creativity and their bravery.

Body Varial

The Body Varial may be the hardest trick. It is similar to a Rock Solid except for an added feature. The rider spins his or her body completely around before grabbing the machine again!

The Rock Solid is a very hard trick. The rider flies along above his or her bike, as Mike Mason is doing here.

Tips for Staying Safe

Tip 1: Remember that all tricks are dangerous, even if professional riders make them look easy.

Tip 2: Make sure your machine is in top working condition.

Tip 3: Always wear the proper safety gear.

Tip 4: Do not go riding alone. You will need help if you hurt yourself.

Tip 5: Make sure your parents know where you are.

Tip 6: Look for a freestyle park near you where you can ride safely.

Tip 7: Take lessons or get advice from more experienced riders.

Tip 8: Start by learning the easiest tricks.

Tip 9: Do not attempt a trick until you feel certain you can do it safely.

Tip 10: Know how to save yourself if a trick is not working.

Glossary

fender (FEN-der) A guard over the wheel of a motorcycle.

foot peg (FUT PEG) The part of the motorcycle where the rider rests his or her foot while riding. There is a foot peg on each side of the motorcycle.

grab holes (GRAB HOHLZ) The holes cut into the motorcycle on each side just below the seat. The rider grabs them while performing tricks such as the Superman Seat Grab.

handstand (HAND-stand) The act of supporting the body on the hands with the arms extended and the body and legs sticking straight up.

professional (pruh-FESH-nul) Someone who is paid for what he or she does.

ramps (RAMPS) Sloping platforms.

rhythm sections (RIH-thum SEK-shunz) Closely spaced series of large bumps that are the same size on racetracks.

signature (SIG-nuh-cher) Something that is especially connected with a person and serves to identify them.

stadiums (STAY-dee-umz) Large buildings for sports events surrounded by rising rows of seats for fans. A stadium usually does not have a roof.

suicidal (soo-uh-SY-dul) Very dangerous.

tabletops (TAY-bul-tops) Large bumps on racetracks that are wide and flat on top.

whoops (HOOPS) A series of small, closely spaced bumps on a racetrack.

Index

Web Sites

Due to the changing nature of Internet links, PowerKids Press has developed an online list of Web sites related to the subject of this book. This site is updated regularly. Please use this link to access the list:

www.powerkidslinks.com/motoc/tips/